THE ITCH OF THE GOLDEN NIT

Book Text by Dave Ingham

School was over, and an amazing, fantastic and rather itchy adventure was about to begin.

Not that Beanie would know, as he picked a lone path through gaggles of screaming school kids.

You see, Beanie didn't have lots of friends – unlike his big sister BERYL.

He was never picked for the school football team like the other boys ... No one really noticed him. He was plain old Beanie.

Beanie stopped by the corner shop, and there he saw it ... 'It's the new *10 Heart Hero*!' It was his number one superhero comic.

How he wished he were like 10 Heart ... Everyone would notice him then. Oh yes, he'd fight evil and get picked for the school football team! He'd be a somebody, not a nobody!

Beanie was too busy reading his comic to notice Mum and Dad looking up at the dim, spluttering sun. The newspapers said it was going out. It could really mean the end of the world – even the universe!

Suddenly a massive spaceship parked above them! An alien called Evil Stella and her sidekick Fireboy dangled down.

'I am Evil Stella – give me my Golden Nit!' Stella demanded. Mum and Dad only gave to Children in Need, and anyway they didn't have a clue about any nit.

So Evil Stella shrank them both with Electric Bubbles. 'Seize them, Fireball!' she shouted at Fireboy. She needed that Golden Nit so she could rule the universe, and she was convinced Beanie's Mum and Dad had it.

Fireboy scooped Mum and Dad up like two little dolls, but very gently – he wasn't evil like Stella. In fact he was getting sick of her getting his name wrong and shouting at him all the time.

As quickly as they arrived, Evil Stella and Fireboy blasted into space with their captives. 'Mwahahahahaaaaa!!'

Back in the house, Beanie couldn't believe his eyes when his big sister turned up. She'd been shrunk by electric bubbles too! 'This is SO not happening to me!!!!' Beryl screamed. Beanie tried not to giggle.

When Beanie heard that Mum and Dad had been shrunk and taken by actual aliens, he knew he needed help – Superhero help!

Unfortunately all the superheroes were either on holiday or too busy saving the galaxy.

'We'll have to save them ourselves!' said Beanie. So he phoned an ad in the back of his comic. 'All a superhero needs are pants, gadgets and a heart!'

Beanie and his shrunken sister were quickly taken by dinosaur taxi to Super Co the Superhero Superstore.

But they could only enter Super Co with Superhero names. 'ENTER – BLEND-IN BOY and SHOUTY BERYL!' announced President Pinky the three-eyed doorman. They were in ...

WOW! What a shop! There was Mothman, Stretchy McStretch, Smelly Melon and Electro Boy ... In fact all kinds of superheroes flew amongst the aisles with their bulging trolleys. Gadgets of all shapes and sizes filled the shelves.

Shouty Beryl just had to shop – she loved the Freeze Ray ... adored the Rocket Jeans ... and the Laser Lip Gloss was a must-have!

After an accident with a Sonic Football, Blend-In Boy had to settle for a pair of Blend-In Pants.

'You're 10 Heart Hero!' Beanie shouted in amazement as he looked at the man working the checkout. Not exactly a job for a Galaxy-saving Superhero ... On hearing their Mum and Dad had been shrunk and taken away, 10 Heart Hero knew straight away it was Evil Stella. She planned to rule the universe with the Golden Nit!

THE GOLDEN NIT!!!!! Suddenly the store was filled with a golden light. Everyone staggered backwards as the Golden Nit rose from Beanie's hair! He had been hiding there for days and now he needed a hero to take him to his home – the sun. 'I am the flame that ignites the sun, so if you don't get me home the universe is kaput!'

There was only one superhero for the job ... Blend-In Boy! 'WHAT??!!' Beanie didn't want to be Blend-In Boy anymore. He just wanted his Mum and Dad back!

'Looks like someone needs a hero!' said 10 Heart Hero as he leapt over his checkout. He'd take them all to the sun in his rainbow spaceship – easy!

As they raced across the galaxy towards the sun, who should be on their tail but Evil Stella! Using her cunning Nit Nav, she discovered that Beanie had the Golden Nit – and nothing was going to stop her from getting it back!

'Two parents for one nit! Then I can get on with ruling the universe ... deal?' shouted Evil Stella as she chased them, firing Full Fat Custard Torpedoes. Things were getting sticky!

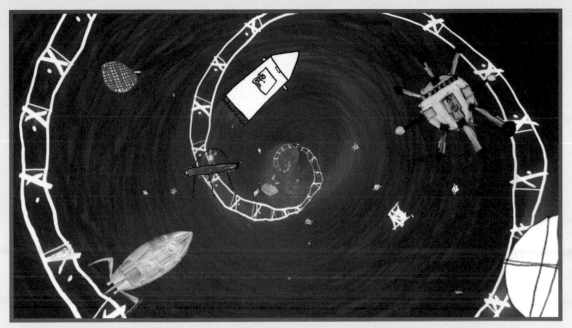

Just as Evil Stella was about to catch them, the Rainbow Spaceship got sucked into another dimension – WOOOOOOAH!

... around and around and around, until they landed in a strange ocean with a PLOP!

Captain Iron Ears and his stinky crew pulled them from the waves. The Smelly Pirates loved singing silly sea shanties and firing cannon balls at each other.

The Captain made a deal with Beanie. In return for taking them up the Scary Hairy River to find the sun, Beanie had to rescue the Captain's Golden Fish Finger from the terrible Moody Mermaids.

Beanie's knees knocked as he jumped overboard and activated his Blend-In Pants, transforming him into a food inspector from the Cornish Council!

His cunning disguise worked, and he tricked the Moody Mermaids into handing over the Golden Fish Finger, telling them it was off and needed testing.

But then the Moody Mermaids spotted the Golden Nit under his hat and tried to grab it. Beanie just managed to escape!

With the Golden Fishfinger safely in Captain Iron Ears's treasure chest, our heroes voyaged up the Scary Hairy River. It was a dark, foreboding place. The further they went, the scarier and hairier things got ...

Then 10 Heart Hero admitted the terrible truth. 'For ten minutes every week I'm cursed with being bad. That's why I lost my job as a superhero.' The only problem was, he hadn't been bad yet this week ...

Little did they know that Stella was following their every move on her Nit Nav. That Golden Nit would soon be hers! 'And everyone will know it's all about me!' she screamed.

The good ship Tanky Boon ran aground, stuck in the stinky, murky river.

Thankfully, 10 Heart Hero transformed his spaceship into a canoe, so that they could continue their journey to the sun. Sadly Captain Iron Ears couldn't join them ... he needed a poo!

Through a dark, dank jungle they paddled, until there, spluttering dimly above them, they saw the sun ... Were they too late to save it?

Suddenly they were surrounded by Frazzle McGover, Ugly Goonie, Dr Dococo and Spanish Michelle ... In fact, all the super villains in the universe were closing in on them! There could only be one person behind this ...

Rainbow
Canoe

... EVIL STELLA! 'Mwahahahaaaaa! Give me the Golden Nit!' she cried, offering Beanie his tiny parents in return.

As bad luck would have it, 10 Heart Hero picked this moment to turn evil, grabbing the Golden Nit from Beanie!

But before he could give the Golden Nit to Evil Stella, KERPOW! Beryl blasted at him with her laser lip gloss! Stella commanded everyone to 'GET THAT NIT!'

The Golden Nit curled himself into a tight ball. Beanie really needed to show off his footie skills now!

Beryl and Mum and Dad cheered him on. What a player! 'Get him Fireface!' ordered Evil Stella.

Beanie was cornered! He got tackled ... He couldn't get the nit back!

... until Fireboy stepped forward ... He'd had enough of Evil Stella ordering him around! He passed the Golden Nit back to Beanie.

Beanie had one chance – one kick to save the universe ... 'Goodbye Beanie!' the Golden Nit shouted as he hurtled towards the dying sun.

'Plopping heck! Noooooooooo!!!' screamed Evil Stella.

Like a light bulb being switched on, the sun shone brightly down on everyone once more. What a shot! Beanie had saved the universe! 'Our Beanie's a hero!' shouted Dad.

Beanie had got his Mum and Dad back. He was even pleased to have a big sister again, though she was still shouty.

10 Heart Hero turned his spaceship into an icecream van and they all celebrated with Happy Hero Cones.

Back at school, things were looking up. 'BEANIE! BEANIE! BEANIE!'

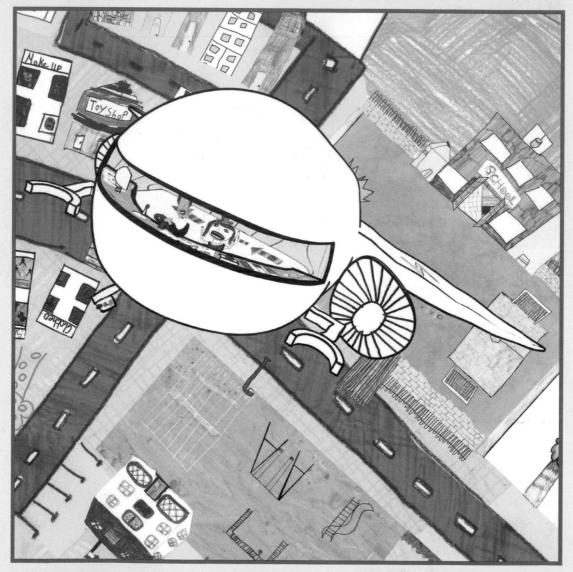

As for Evil Stella and 10 Heart Hero? Well that's a whole different story ...
'Mwahahahahahaaaa!'